JUN - - 2024

RACHEL FRIEDMAN
Breaks the Rules

Also by Sarah Kapit

Get a Grip, Vivy Cohen!

The Many Mysteries of the Finkel Family

Second Chance Summer

RACHEL FRIEDMAN

BREAKS THE RULES

SARAH KAPIT

ILLUSTRATED BY GENEVIEVE KOTE

HENRY HOLT AND COMPANY

New York

Henry Holt and Company, *Publishers since 1866*

Henry Holt® is a registered trademark of Macmillan Publishing Group, LLC

120 Broadway, New York, NY 10271 • mackids.com

Our books may be purchased in bulk for promotional, educational, or business
use. Please contact your local bookseller or the Macmillan Corporate and
Premium Sales Department at (800) 221-7945 ext. 5442 or by email at
MacmillanSpecialMarkets@macmillan.com.

Library of Congress Cataloging-in-Publication Data

Names: Kapit, Sarah, author. | Kote, Genevieve, illustrator.
Title: Rachel Friedman breaks the rules / Sarah Kapit ; [illustrations by
Genevieve Kote].
Description: First edition. | New York : Henry Holt Books for Young Readers,
2024. | Audience: Ages 5–9. | Audience: Grades 2–3. | Summary: "Rachel
is not one for rules, but when a meet-and-greet with her favorite gymnast
is at risk, she must be on her best behavior, especially at synagogue"—
Provided by publisher.
Identifiers: LCCN 2023029071 | ISBN 9781250880932 (hardcover)
Subjects: CYAC: Attention-deficit hyperactivity disorder—Fiction. | Rules—
Fiction. | Jews—United States—Fiction.
Classification: LCC PZ7.1.K32 Rac 2024 | DDC [Fic]—dc23
LC record available at https://lccn.loc.gov/2023029071

First edition, 2024
Book design by Abby Granata
Printed in the United States of America by Lakeside Book Company,
Crawfordsville, Indiana

ISBN 978-1-250-88093-2 (hardcover)
1 3 5 7 9 10 8 6 4 2

ISBN 978-1-250-88092-5 (paperback)
1 3 5 7 9 10 8 6 4 2

To Grandpa Charlie

CHAPTER 1

The Rules at Shul

Up on the bimah, the rabbi talks. In my head, I run through my new gymnastics routine. I finish a perfect cartwheel, then go straight into a back handspring. At the end of the routine, I strike a winning pose. I nailed it!

Everyone cheers for me. I can see my best friend, Maya, and my dad and my brother and Coach Kayla and even my favorite gymnast, Holly Luna. Holly walks toward me, her black hair tied back in her famous ponytail. She is going to talk to me and tell me how awesome I am, and . . . and . . .

"Rachel! Arms down!" Dad whispers to me.

Oops. I guess for a moment I forgot that I'm not really at the gym, with my coach and friends cheering me on. Nope! Instead, I am sitting in a hard bench at shul. *Shul* is Yiddish for *synagogue*.

Some people also say *temple*. But it doesn't matter what you call it. Going to shul is BORING.

Don't get me wrong. I really love being Jewish.

I eat kasha varnishkas and matzo ball soup. Yum!

I dress up every year for Purim. Last year, I was a pirate. Ahoy!

And, best of all, when it's time for Hanukkah, I get eight presents over eight nights. Hooray!

But services at shul are not even a little bit fun. That's because there are too many rules for what you're supposed to do at shul—and what you're not supposed to do. Most of the rules aren't written down anywhere, but everyone knows that you have to follow them.

Here are some of the worst ones:

- Don't eat during services in the sanctuary (even when you're really, really hungry).
- Keep quiet while the rabbi talks (and the rabbi always talks).
- Never ever play tag in the hallways (or hide-and-go-seek).
- Don't do cartwheels anywhere in the building (even though I am super good at them).

All the little rules add up to one big rule:

- Don't have any fun.

Now do you see why I don't like going to shul?

Today, Dad and I are at Shabbat evening services. Shabbat is a Jewish holiday that happens every week, which makes it not a very exciting holiday, in my opinion.

Shabbat begins on Friday night and ends on Saturday night, so it's not even like I get to take a day off from school. (That would make Shabbat much, much better.)

Some people go to Shabbat services every Friday, but not us. We go once or twice a month. My dad says every family has their own way of being Jewish, and this is our way.

Unluckily for me, today is one of the days we're at Friday night services. I don't think it's fair that I have to go tonight, because my big brother, Aaron, isn't here. He's away on an overnight trip with his math team. Lucky him!

But Dad thought today would be a good night for services. So I have to sit still while Rabbi Ellen talks and talks and talks some more. I don't know what she's talking about. I just wish she could finish a little faster. I have ADHD, so paying attention is sometimes hard for me. Also, Rabbi Ellen is talking about stuff that I don't really understand. I just want the service to be over so I can have dessert!

Up in the second row, Mr. Goldman snores. He must have trouble paying attention, too. I'm pretty sure sleeping in shul is against the rules, but no one is scolding him. I guess grown-ups can get away with breaking the rules. So unfair.

Well, if he can sleep while the rabbi talks, then maybe I can break the rules, too.

I smile.

CHAPTER 2
Crash Landing

I don't want to break the rules too badly—I just want to break them a little. I just want to do something—anything!—besides sitting still and being quiet. I *hate* sitting still and being quiet. So I look around the sanctuary, searching for a fun thing to do. Soon I find it: the program. The program is a piece of paper that someone passes out at the beginning of

every service. I don't know why. They just do. I don't read the program, because that would be super boring. Lucky for me, I can use the piece of paper for something else. I am going to make an airplane.

Before I begin, I peek at Dad. He is staring at the words in his prayer book, but he has not turned a single page in the last ten minutes. Really, he looks only a little more awake than snoring Mr. Goldman. I don't think he'll notice if I decide to break the rules a little. So I fold the program into the nose of an airplane. Next, I give the plane wide wings and a narrow tail.

When I finish, I smile. I did a great job, and my plane is absolutely fantabulous.

Now I just need to test it out. I *know* that it will work. I just know it.

I know I shouldn't do it. Not now. Not here in synagogue, with all the grown-ups and their rules.

But I want to. My very bestest friend in the whole world, Maya, is sitting two rows in front of me. Even though I can't see her face, I know she's bored just like me. I can send my airplane to her as a gift! That will make her super happy. It's practically my job as her best friend.

If I do it quickly enough, no one will notice. I look at Dad again. He's still not reading his prayer book and, more important, not paying any attention to me.

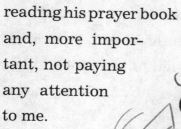

I position the plane. I pull my arm back and take aim at Maya's head. Finally, I let the airplane go. It flies!

My plane soars all the way over Maya's head and into the next row. The plane goes into a steep dive, sort of like me when I make a mistake on the balance beam.

And then my plane lands straight on Mr. Goldman's bald head.

Whoops, whoops, and more whoops. I missed big-time, and that means big-time trouble.

All of a sudden, Mr. Goldman wakes up. He makes a noise that sounds like an elephant clearing her throat.

"What?" he says. He is very, very loud. Definitely loud enough for everyone in the sanctuary to hear. Even Rabbi Ellen stops talking about whatever.

Mr. Goldman snaps his head around

and scowls at everyone. He is very good at scowling.

I make myself really small so he can't see me. If he could, I'm sure he would know that I am so, so guilty. But I can't hide from Dad.

Dad isn't half asleep now. He is most definitely awake. After he runs a hand through his hair, he gives me a stern look.

"Rachel Friedman, you are in trouble," he says.

I know. But then I remember the noise

Mr. Goldman made when the plane crashed into him, and I giggle. I giggle a lot. Dad gives me another look, but that just makes me laugh even more.

Now everyone knows it was me. People point and stare. I even hear some soft laughing sounds. Maya turns around and gives me a thumbs-up.

Some things are worth getting in a little trouble.

CHAPTER 3

Two Cups of Flour

When Dad said I was in trouble, he meant it. Now I have to clean my cat Cookie's litter box for two whole weeks. Big yuck! I love Cookie, but I do not like her poop even a little bit.

At least one good thing is happening today: Maya and her moms are coming over for Shabbat dinner! Well, since it's Saturday now, I guess it's an after-Shabbat dinner. But that doesn't matter. The important part is that Maya and I are going to make challah. And Dad is helping a little.

Whenever I make challah, I follow the recipe. A recipe is a list of rules about how to make food—in this case, challah. The first time I made challah, I didn't follow the rules the right way. When it said "two cups of flour," I thought that meant I should get out one of our drinking cups. I poured two whole cups in the batter, just like the recipe said. I didn't know that there were special cups just for measuring stuff. The people who write recipes should be more specific about this, in my opinion. Anyway, this mistake turned out to be a very, very big problem. When I tried to mix the dough, all the flour clogged up our mixer and made a mess.

So now I know that it is important to follow all the instructions.

When I start to make the challah, I am very careful. I pour flour into the measuring cup while Dad watches me. He doesn't really need to do that, but I guess he wants to make sure that everything goes right.

Next comes my very favorite part — cracking the eggs. Maya doesn't like doing this, because if you mess up, then your hands get all sticky and gross. But I love it. I grab an egg and knock it against the edge of the counter.

CRACK!

I pull the eggshell apart above the bowl, and the egg yolk whooshes straight into it. It is perfect and round. I smile and then crack three more eggs.

Now it's time to mix everything. Dad flips the switch, and the ingredients swirl around together in the mixer. When we pull the bowl out, everything is nice and doughy.

The next part is really, really boring. We have to wait for the dough to get bigger. Before we can braid the dough into a loaf, it has to get bigger.

Who wants to wait around and watch dough sit in a bowl? Not me!

So I grab Maya's arm.

"Let's have fun," I say.

CHAPTER 4
Breaking a Rule

Maya and I race up to my room so we can have best-friend time. Dad can make sure that the challah dough doesn't explode or anything. (Not that it's going to do anything interesting like that!)

I turn on my computer while Maya lounges on the floor. There are very important things for us to do—like watching videos of Holly Luna online. Holly is the most fantabulous gymnast in the whole wide world. Both of us want to be just like Holly when we grow up.

For now, it would be super awesome just to meet Holly. The good news is, she's coming to our town in three weeks for a gymnastics show! At the end of the show, some fans will get to meet her. Ever since we found out about it, Maya and I have been on a mission. We're trying to convince our parents to buy tickets for us.

"I can't wait to meet her," Maya says. "Can. Not!"

"Me neither. We should plan the next step of our mission! I've asked Dad about it, but he hasn't said yes for sure. I think maybe I should do something extra dramatic, just to show him how much I want to go. Maybe I can draw a sign and put it up in the living room! What do you think? What did your moms say about it?"

At that, Maya looks like she's about ready to explode.

"I've been dying to tell you . . . my moms bought tickets for the show yesterday. So mission accomplished for me!"

What? This is big, big news.

"You're going to meet Holly?!" I squeal, and give my best friend a big hug.

"Yep! Can you believe it? So awesome!"

"Awesome," I repeat.

Maybe I'm a little less enthusiastic than Maya, but who can blame me?

I am happy for her. Really, I am. But if I'm being honest, then I have to admit that I'm just a teeny bit jealous. I've asked Dad about getting tickets a million times. A trillion times! But he always just says "Maybe." Maybe if the schedule works out. Maybe if I do chores and be good and stuff. Blah, blah, blah. Now Maya gets to go, and she might go without me. If that happens, it will be the unfairest thing in the whole entire universe.

Maya pats me on the arm. "We'll convince your dad," she assures me. "Though I don't know if making a sign is the best idea."

She's probably right. I sigh, but I try to smile for Maya.

"Yeah. I'll convince him."

"Shake on it?" she asks.

I smile again, and this time it's a real smile, not a for-show smile. Whenever Maya and I make a promise to each other, we do our special best-friend handshake. No one knows how to do it except for us.

Just as Maya and I finish doing our handshake, Dad calls us back into the kitchen. The challah dough is ready for us! Now I have something to think about besides Holly and Maya and how the world (and Dad) is totally unfair.

I grin when I see our big, puffy ball of dough. It's going to taste so good!

I look at it. Maybe there's something we can do to make it even better. I look around the kitchen and see a jar of peanut butter sitting on the counter. Yes!

I point. "Can we add that to the dough?" I ask Dad.

"Peanut butter and challah? I don't know about that."

Dad can be boring sometimes. Actually, he can be boring a lot of the time.

"You always say that peanut butter makes everything better," I remind him.

"I guess we can give it a try."

Maya braids the dough. She is really good at braiding, and now the loaf looks so pretty. Once she's done, I use a spoon to put little bits of peanut butter in between the creases of the braid. When I'm done, I lick the peanut butter off the spoon. Yum!

"Here's to an experiment," Dad says.

Sometimes, even Dad is okay with breaking the rules a little.

CHAPTER 5

The Agreement

Big discovery! It turns out that peanut butter challah is yummy—even better than regular challah. Everyone else thinks so, too.

I eat three pieces of challah. Dad says I won't have room for the rest of my dinner after so much challah, but I prove him wrong. I finish every single bit of chicken and the piece of noodle kugel on my plate.

Soon we get to the part of Shabbat where the grown-ups talk with each other. Dad and Maya's moms talk soooo much whenever they're together. I squirm in my seat. I need something to do—something fun and fabulous!

Luckily, my brother came home from his math thing, and now he's here for dinner. I think it's time to welcome him back.

I spot a leftover piece of challah and smile. I grab the challah and squish it into a ball. Then I throw it straight across the table at Aaron's chest. "Hey!" he yelps.

"Gotcha!"

Dad stops talking in the middle of a sentence and glances over at me. He presses his fingers to his head. "Rachel, you know that throwing things at your brother is against the rules. So is wasting food."

I pout. "Well, I don't like the rules very much."

"I am well aware of that, but you still have to follow them," Dad says.

"But that's no fun at all!"

Dad laughs, but he's still wearing his serious face. "I'll tell you what, Rachey. I know you really want to meet this Holly Lara—"

"Holly Luna!" I interrupt.

Dad is so silly. How does he not know Holly's name?

"Right," he says. "Holly Luna. So how

about this? You follow the rules for one whole week. And I do mean every single rule, even the ones you don't like very much. If you can do it, I will buy tickets so that you can meet Holly."

Maya turns to me and flashes a thumbs-up. This is exactly what we wanted! I didn't even have to make a sign or anything.

"Really?" I squeak.

"Really," Dad says.

That settles it. Maybe I don't like a lot of the rules. Or most of them, really. But if there's a chance for me to meet Holly and tell her how awesome she is, then I have to take it. Even if I'm in for one very, very boring week.

"Okay. I'll do it!"

Dad holds out a hand, and we shake on it.

Not a superspecial friendship handshake—just a boring grown-up handshake. Maya claps.

Aaron smirks. "Good luck, Rachey-kins. You'll need it."

Ever since Aaron turned thirteen and had his bar mitzvah this year, he thinks he's a grown-up. (For the record, he definitely isn't. He's just annoying!)

I start to stick my tongue out at him,

but then I remember that sticking out my tongue at people is probably Against the Rules. So I can't.

Dad frowns at my brother. "Don't be mean to your sister." Then he turns to me. "I know you can do this, Rachel."

I give my dad a thumbs-up, but my stomach still feels jittery. I hate to admit it, but Aaron's right. This is going to be hard.

Really, really hard.

CHAPTER 6

Being (Mostly) Good

For the next few days, I am good. I am so, so good. Nobody in the whole history of the world has ever been as good as me!

I go to bed on time every single night. I don't do any cartwheels in the kitchen (or the dining room). I even scoop up Cookie's poop when it's Aaron's turn. Someone should give me an award for all this.

Aaron tries to make everything harder for me because he is mean like that. On Monday, he tosses me a bread roll at dinner. I catch it. I want to throw it back at him, but that would be Against the Rules. So I don't. I just take a big bite of my roll and smile my very sweetest smile at Aaron.

"Thank you very much," I say to him. "It was so nice of you to give me your food."

On Tuesday, Aaron tells me that the ice-cream truck is only a few blocks away, and I almost run straight out the door. Just in time, I remember that I am not supposed to cross the street without an adult. That is also Against the Rules. So I wait until Dad takes me. We get there

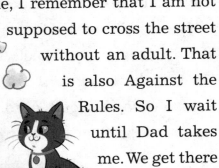

late and have to
wait in line a really
long time, but I end
up with a chocolate ice-
cream cone. Yum!

On Wednesday, Aaron is
the absolute worst. After I finish
my homework, we play Monopoly together.
(I did all my homework early because I am
Following the Rules.) Aaron says he didn't
cheat, but I can see him sneaking purple
fifty-dollar bills into his stack. I want to
yell at him, but that would be Against the
Rules. I have to show Dad that I can follow
the rules. Then I can meet Holly Luna and
get her autograph and show her my perfect cartwheels.

Also, I win the game anyway. Ha! Even
cheating can't beat my awesome Monopoly
skills.

By the time Thursday comes around, I start to think that I can really do it. After all, there are just two days left. That's hardly anything at all. Since I started trying to follow the rules, it's gotten much easier. Even if it is a little boring. I so wish I could sneak pepper into Aaron's cereal just once!

I start my homework the exact moment I get home. Once I'm done, I go outside. Dad set up a bunch of mats for me in the garage so I can practice gymnastics whenever I want.

I practice my somersaults, cartwheels, and handsprings. I want to get my skills perfect for when I meet Holly Luna. But then my hands start to feel sore, so I take a break. Even Holly takes breaks sometimes. Probably. Maybe I'll ask when I meet her.

So I go into the house for a cup of raspberry lemonade. That's when I notice

something. Something Very Important. The front door is already open.

The door is not supposed to be open. That is definitely Against the Rules. And this rule isn't like most other rules. This rule actually makes sense. Cookie is not allowed to go outside because outside there are cars and other things that are dangerous for cats.

My forehead starts to get all sweaty.

"Cookie!" I call. "Where are you?"

CHAPTER 7

The Search for Cookie

I try my best not to panic. Even though Cookie loves me more than she loves anyone else, obviously, she does her own thing all the time. What does she do when she's not with me? I've always wondered about that. I even thought about getting a secret camera to follow her around. But Dad says it would be rude to spy.

Luckily, I know her favorite hiding places.

I check behind the couch. No Cookie.

I check inside the laundry basket. No Cookie.

I check underneath my bed. No Cookie. (But I do find my second-favorite pen.)

This is not right. This is not right at all.

"Treat!" I call out. "Cookie! I have very yummy food for you."

Cookie does not know many words. In fact, I don't think she even knows that her name is Cookie. But she knows the word *treat* and the word *food*. If she's here, she should come racing over, demanding to be fed. I wait to hear the jingling sound of her bells as she rushes toward me.

But I don't. I don't hear anything besides the hum of the refrigerator. So I run through the house, calling, "Treat! Treat! Treat!"

I get louder and louder as I run. There are still no signs of Cookie.

"Come here!" I try. "Please!"

The more I yell, the more panicked I get. My palms are gross and sweaty, and I can feel my heart thumping loudly in my chest.

No matter how many times I say the magic words, Cookie does not come to me. There is only one explanation: Cookie is not here in the house. At all.

Aaron isn't here, either. He is supposed to be watching me while Dad goes and does boring grown-up stuff, but I guess he left. *Aaron* broke the rules! I hope he gets into so much trouble for that. It would serve him right.

But that's not the most important thing right now. Cookie needs to be rescued. And there is only one person in the whole world who can do it: me.

I could try calling Dad or Aaron on the phone, but that would take too much time. I don't have time to talk with them. Cookie needs me! I will not let her down.

I grab a bag of kitty treats and stuff it in my pocket. The treats are salmon flavored, which is Cookie's favorite. Then I put on my running shoes.

"I'm coming for you, Cookie!"

CHAPTER 8
The Rescue

I check every single bush in our front yard, but I can't find Cookie anywhere. She isn't in Ms. Nelson's front yard, either.

Next, I decide to check the Wellses' porch, even though Mr. Wells is a big old meanie. No Cookie there, either.

Then I see it—a flash of black-and-white fur! Cookie is across the street. I think she ran right into a bush.

Poor Cookie! She must be so scared all by herself. I have to help her before something bad comes along, like a coyote or a truck or a cat-hating supervillain. I can't wait for anyone else to help. I am Cookie's number one person, and this is *my* job.

Crossing the street without a grown-up (or Aaron) is definitely Against the Rules. I know it is . . . but I don't care. Cookie is way more important than any stupid rule.

Besides, this is obviously one of those

times when a rule makes no sense. I think it's totally fair for me to bend the rule a little, just this once. For Cookie. Dad will understand when I explain everything to him. I'm sure of it. Well, almost sure. But there's no time for me to worry about that too much. I have a cat to save.

I race across the street. I know I should cross at the crosswalk, but I don't have time! Besides, our street isn't big or dangerous. Most people drive soooo slowly, which is very annoying when I'm in the car and I want Dad to go faster.

Moving as quickly as I can, I race toward the bush where I saw the flash of fur.

Almost there! Now I just need to leap over a big pile of leaves.

I extend my legs and take off for my leap. I soar through the air, almost like a cat myself.

But I make a mistake. Usually, I'm a fabulous leaper. Coach Kayla always says so. But when I practice leaps for gymnastics, I'm barefoot. Now I'm wearing big, clunky sneakers. And the leaf pile is really, really tall. Maybe if I wasn't wearing shoes, I could have made it, but not now. I don't get enough height on the leap.

So I fall.

CHAPTER 9
The Fall

I plummet straight into the pile of dirty, soggy leaves.

"Yuck!" I say.

When I pick myself up, I realize that there's another problem. The pile of leaves isn't just leaves. There's also a slimy goop.

Slimy *brown* goop.

I have fallen into a pile of dog poop. And

let me tell you, dog poop is even stinkier than cat poop.

Now the stinkiness is all over me. I want to go home and take a bubble bath so I can get rid of it for good. But I can't. I still have to save Cookie. Even though I stink, I am not going to let her down!

But I can't find her. I check under the bush, but she isn't there anymore. She could have gone anywhere while I was being poop-bombed!

"Cookie!" I call out. I don't really expect her to respond, but I try anyway.

Thanks to some kind of miracle, a high-pitched meow calls back to me. I can barely hear it over the buzzing lawn mower next door, but it's Cookie! I know it is.

I don't know where she is exactly, but she must be close. So I follow the sound down the driveway. And then . . .

"Cookie!"

There she is, all squished up beneath a plastic slide. Less than ten feet away, a ginormous dog is barking loudly. That mean dog must be scaring Cookie.

"Be quiet!" I tell the dog. "And go away!"

I run over to Cookie and scoop her up in my arms. She purrs and buries her head in my hands. She's so happy to see me that she doesn't even claw at me like she usually does when I pick her up.

"You were a very bad girl! Why didn't you just stay at home, where you can eat treats and be safe?"

She doesn't answer, but her ears perk up at the word *treats*. I dig through my pockets for the baggie I brought with me, but I can't find it. I must have dropped it when I fell.

"I'll give you a treat later," I promise. "As soon as we get home."

Cookie whines. I'm pretty sure she doesn't understand the word *later*. She starts squirming in my arms, but I hold on supertight.

I make extra sure to check the street for cars before I cross, just like Dad always tells me to do. Maybe I broke the rules, technically speaking, but I have done my best to stay safe! Besides, everything I did was for Cookie.

Soon, we reach our house. Dad's car is now in the driveway, and Dad himself stands in the front door. Parts of his hair are sticking up in a funny way, and his face has turned very, very red.

"Rachel, thank goodness!" he says. "Where were you? And why do you smell like number two?"

I hold out Cookie, as if to explain.

Dad sighs. "Come inside."

CHAPTER 10
Cleaning Up

66 . . . So that's how I saved Cookie!" I say.

I tried to keep my story short, since Dad is being weird. But, well, I had to make sure to explain how I was totally a hero.

Cookie meows, so she obviously agrees that I did an amazing thing. She rubs her head against the couch, which means she is a happy cat. Dad rubs his eyes, which means he is a not-happy dad.

"Maybe you had better clean up," Dad suggests.

I almost don't notice the icky poop smell anymore, but cleaning up sounds like a good idea to me. I race toward the stairs. On my way, I run into Aaron and his friend Cole. Aaron has a lot of friends. Most of them are really dorky like he is. Cole is Aaron's very best friend, like Maya is to me. Just like Aaron, Cole can be very, very annoying. And I mean *very*.

"You stink!" Aaron says. "Did you fall into a litter box or something?"

"Actually, it was a pile of leaves with

dog poop," I say. I'm not embarrassed or anything. I got poop-ified while I was saving Cookie. Besides, I'm not the only gross smell around here. Something else smells bad. "You stink, too!"

Both Aaron and Cole look gross and sweaty. Aaron's curly hair is wet and sticks to his forehead. I wrinkle my nose at them.

"Well, at least our stench doesn't come from poop," Aaron says. "We were riding our bikes to the comic store. This is the smell of intense exercise, thank you very much."

Frowning, I think back to the open front door—the door that allowed Cookie to make her escape. I turn to my brother and point a finger at him.

"You left the door open!"

"No, I didn't. I know better than that," Aaron says.

"You did too!"

Aaron gets ready to respond, but Cole speaks first. "Uh. Actually, I think I may have left the door open before we went out. I needed to run back and get my helmet. Sorry."

Sorry? That's not good enough. Poor Cookie was almost hurt because of Cole and his mistake.

"You hurt Cookie," I tell him. "She escaped the house and ran across the street, and then I had to save her! She could have been eaten!"

Cole looks down at his dirty sneakers. His face is really red. "I'm sorry. Really, really sorry."

I cross my arms over my chest. "I think Cole should be punished for what he did."

Aaron rolls his eyes. "That's not your job. Besides, smelling you is punishment enough."

Cole quietly snickers at that. I stick my tongue out at them. But Aaron is right about me stinking, so I go off to clean myself. As I walk into the bathroom, I keep my head held high.

Maybe I am stinky, but I am also a hero!

CHAPTER 11
The Punishment

I change into my favorite leggings and T-shirt once I'm done cleaning up. The shirt reads I'M NOT BOSSY IF I'M RIGHT in glittery pink letters. I think I deserve to wear it right now.

So I guess I have to talk with Dad. He made it sound like it was really important.

"You're in big trouble," Aaron tells me once I arrive downstairs.

What? That can't be right! I saved Cookie. Me! Okay, maybe I did break Dad's rule about not crossing the street by myself. But I had a very, very good reason for breaking the rule. Heroes don't get in trouble for breaking the rules. Or at least they shouldn't.

Aaron must be wrong, just like usual. I make a face at him while I march into the kitchen. I think I deserve an actual cookie after saving cat Cookie. While I munch on my chocolate chip cookie, Dad comes in.

"We need to talk," he says.

Uh-oh. In my eight whole years of experience, nothing good ever comes after those four words. I shove another cookie into my mouth to avoid saying anything, but Dad gives me a look—his Serious Face.

"Rachey. Honey. You broke the rules again, and it really scared me."

I finish chewing the cookie too fast, and it makes my stomach feel funny. But that doesn't matter. I need to defend myself.

"Aaron broke the rules, too!" I point out.

"Oh, I've talked to Aaron," Dad says. He scowls, and for a moment—just a teeny second—I feel a little sorry for my brother. "But we're not talking about him right now. We're talking about you."

"I only crossed the street for Cookie! She needed me."

"I understand. But you could have gotten hurt crossing the street all by yourself."

"I was careful," I say, even though I maybe wasn't the most careful.

Dad sighs and pushes a curly strand of hair away from his glasses. "We've discussed this before, Rachel. You know the rule."

Ugh! I know. Why is he being so annoying? Maybe if I show him that I'm really, really sorry, he'll let it go.

"I won't ever cross the street by myself ever again. Pinkie swear!" I say. I hold out my pinkie to show that I mean it.

Dad nods and locks pinkies with me. "Cool beans."

I groan. Dad is the only person in the whole wide world who says stuff like "cool beans." That is actually a very uncool thing to say. Well, at least this means I'm not in any more trouble. Right?

"I know it was a tough situation for you. I get it," Dad goes on. "But, Rachey, when I tell you that you need to follow the rules, I mean it. All the rules, not just the ones you happen to like."

"But . . . but Cookie was in danger!" I protest.

"Maybe so. But, Rachel, *you* also could have been in danger. There's a reason why you're not allowed to cross the street by yourself. When I think about what could have happened . . ."

Dad's words trail off, and he sighs yet again. He gets like this sometimes. Dad once told me that because Mom died when I was a little kid, he has to be Super Dad for us. I think he is already a super dad, but he means something else. He says he needs to work extra hard to keep Aaron and me safe. Most of the time, I don't mind. But every once in a while, it is totally the worst.

"I'm sorry I made a mistake," I say. "Really, really sorry."

"I'm glad to hear it. But you're still cleaning up cat poop all by yourself for another week," Dad says.

I groan, but I know things could be worse.

"And I hate to do this, but you've broken the terms of your agreement," Dad continues. Uh-oh. My heart plummets. "You said you would follow all the rules, no exceptions. So I can't take you to go meet Holly Luna."

What? That's the most unfair thing ever! I was good. I was so, so good for nearly six days, which is almost a whole week. And okay, maybe I did break the rules a little, but I had a very good reason!

I cross my arms and inform Dad of his complete and total unfairness. He nods.

"I'm really sorry, Rachey. But a deal is a deal. You didn't follow all the rules."

"Because of Cookie! She was in danger!" I say for the forty bajillionth time.

"I'm sorry. Maybe you can meet Holly the next time she comes to town."

My throat tightens.

I don't want to meet Holly the next time she comes—that could be a million years from now for all I know! I wanted to meet Holly this very month. Now Maya gets to meet her and I don't. All because of a stupid, stupid deal.

"You are so not cool!" I tell Dad.

"I'm actually okay with not being cool," Dad says. "As long as you're safe."

Ugh! I try and try to change Dad's mind. I promise to clean up cat poop for an extra week. But he doesn't budge.

For almost six long, boring days, I was good. Now all that is completely useless.

Really, there is no point in following the rules.

CHAPTER 12
The Plan

The next day is the worst day in the whole history of days. I have to tell Maya what happened. She agrees with me that Dad is the most unfair person ever.

"Meeting Holly won't be the same without you," she says.

Still, she gets to meet Holly! And I don't. Not fair.

At recess, I make a big, big decision. Following the rules didn't work for me. So why should I even bother with any of it?

Tonight, it's going to be Shabbat again. And I am going to Break the Rules. In a big, big way. I might as well. Dad already said I can't meet Holly Luna. So why not break the rules a little more? Or a lot more?

After six boring days of following all the rules, I am ready to have fun!

I can't wait. And also maybe I feel just a teensy bit nervous. But mostly I can't wait.

I don't know exactly what I am going to do just yet, but I know it has to be big. The biggest! Probably it will end with me scooping up even more cat poop, but that's okay. I have to do this. I have to show Dad and Aaron and everyone else exactly what I think of their stupid rules.

When Dad tells me we're going to Shabbat services tonight, I start coming up with The Plan. It is a very, very good one. I can't concentrate on anything else, no matter how hard I try.

Finally, the time arrives.

The Plan starts going into motion when I dress up for shul. Normally, I would pick one of my very nicest shirts and pants. Even though my nicest shirts and pants are super itchy. Not today, though. I pick out something a whole lot more comfy. Then I put on my longest coat. It goes all the way to my ankles. No one will see my whole outfit until the time is just right. That's part of The Plan.

"You're wearing a nice coat," Dad says.

I smile. "Today is a special day!"

That is not a lie.

Dad drives Aaron and me to shul. When we arrive, I bounce up and down in my seat. Almost time!

"It's great to see you excited about going to synagogue," Dad tells me.

I smile at him. He obviously does not know about The Plan, and I need to keep it that way.

The drive to shul feels like it takes even longer than usual, but finally we get there. This is the moment.

When we arrive in the sanctuary, there are already loads of people. I smile.

I slip off my coat to show everyone my very special outfit: my favorite pair of pajamas. They are bright purple and have starfish all over. I chose these pj's because I am a star. I look *fabulous*. Fantabulous, even!

"Rachel!" Dad says. He has turned very, very red. "I can't believe I'm even asking this question, but why are you wearing your pj's?"

"Because I wanted to," I tell him. That is a very good reason to do anything, in my opinion.

Lots of people walk past us as they find seats. All of them are dressed up in nice clothes. (They're probably itchy. Poor them!) Some of the people stop and stare at me, but no one says anything. Except for Maya, who gives me a big thumbs-up and says, "Nice outfit!"

"Thank you," I say. "You too!"

Actually, her green dress is a little boring. But I want to be nice.

"Next time, maybe I'll wear my puppy pajamas," Maya says.

I grin at her. "That would be so awesome!"

"I don't think so," one of Maya's moms says.

They slip into seats next to ours. Dad still looks not-happy, but his face is no longer bright red. He leans back in his chair.

Dad doesn't know that starfish pajamas are just the beginning of The Plan.

CHAPTER 13

The Plan, Step Two

There are many fabulous things about my pajamas. And one of the most fabulous is this: The pants have pockets! So before we left the house, I snuck a cookie into my pocket. That is Against the Rules. You aren't supposed to eat in the sanctuary.

Of course, you're not supposed to wear pajamas to shul, either, but I did that.

CRINKLE
CRINKLE!!

I take out my cookie and unwrap it. The packaging makes a crinkling sound. It is very, very loud—almost louder than Rabbi Ellen's voice. Aaron looks at me with wide eyes and thin lips.

Silly Aaron! I ignore him and start munching on the cookie. That's part of The Plan. Except . . . I don't think the cookie tastes as yummy as it usually does. Even though it's chocolate chip. Maybe Breaking the Rules is bad for my stomach.

But I am going through with The Plan, so I keep chewing my cookie. I'm halfway done with it when Dad finally lifts his head out of his prayer book and notices me.

Uh-oh.

"Rachel!" he whispers loudly in my ear. "You know better than to eat in shul."

I should probably listen to him. I know that. But, well, I already started eating the cookie, so I might as well finish the job. Right? One of Dad's rules is: *Don't waste food*. Really, if you look at it the right way, I am being good.

I eat more and more of the cookie. Meanwhile, Dad gets redder and redder until I think he's ready to explode. Some people start looking at us in a way that's kind of funny. My stomach does cartwheels. I don't want to admit it, but maybe The Plan wasn't actually one of my best ideas ever. Maybe it was really a bad idea.

Dad runs a hand through his curly hair. His yarmulke—the hat he wears in shul—has fallen off his head and onto the floor. I reach down and pick it up for him, which is very helpful of me. I swallow the last bits of cookie and lick my lips. By now, a whole bunch of people are looking at us.

What should I do? I don't want everyone looking at me while I just sit here! I still have crumbs on my mouth and chin, which is icky.

Hmm. Maybe I can give them a show.

CHAPTER 14

The Grand Finale

My palms are gross and sweaty, but I wipe them off on my pajama pants. I need sturdy hands for The New Plan.

I march over to the center aisle of the sanctuary. Now absolutely everyone is looking at me. That's a bajillion people! Or at least a hundred. Either way, it's too late for me to back out.

So I leap up in the air and launch into a handstand.

I hold the handstand for three seconds before bringing myself right side up again. I can hold a handstand for longer than that, but it doesn't seem like a very good idea right now. Even in my pajamas, I keep perfect form the entire time. If Coach Kayla were here, she'd tell me I did a great job.

Nobody here says that. In fact, nobody says anything. The room is completely silent. And that makes me really, really nervous.

Rabbi Ellen stares at me from the bimah. She isn't talking anymore because I interrupted her rabbi things. Which was very, very bad of me. I know it was.

I get ready for her to tell me that I've been bad, but she doesn't. Actually, she does the weirdest thing ever. Rabbi Ellen

puts her hands together, and she claps. For me!

Then other people do something that's even weirder. They start clapping, too. Everyone is applauding me for breaking the rules!

I want to take a bow like I usually do after

CLAP CLAP CLAP CLAP

a gymnastics performance, but I decide not to. The whole situation isn't like anything that's ever happened before, and I don't really know what I should do. So I stay very, very still.

Finally, the clapping dies down, and I slink back toward my seat. Before I can make it, Rabbi Ellen starts talking again. To me!

"Rachel, can you explain why you did a handstand?" she asks.

I gulp. My skin feels grosser and sweatier than ever. Doing a handstand in front of everyone was easy. But explaining *why* I did a handstand . . . well, that is very, very hard. All of a sudden, I can't remember why I did it. Why did I do any of this—the pajamas, the cookie, the gymnastics?

Since I can't think of a good lie, I decide to tell the truth. "I wanted to break the rules," I say.

Rabbi Ellen nods. "And why did you want to break the rules, Rachel?"

The rabbi asks very good questions. I guess that's part of being a rabbi. It is a little annoying. But since she asked, I will be honest in my answer.

"Because I don't like these rules! They don't make sense," I tell her. "I think I should be able to wear what I want and eat and have fun at shul."

Even though breaking the rules wasn't actually much fun at all. Funny how that works.

"Huh," Rabbi Ellen says. "That's an interesting point of view. I'll take it into consideration."

Wait. *Really?*

Grown-ups are

so weird. I will never ever understand them for as long as I live.

Rabbi Ellen goes back to talking about the Torah. I think that means she's done asking me questions. So I return to my seat. Dad is there to give me his most serious look.

"You, Rachel Friedman, are in trouble."

Yep. I so, so am.

Still. I did The Plan! I did even more than I originally planned, in fact. *And* the rabbi said she would take my point of view into consideration. I call that a win, even if I didn't always feel very winner-ish while everything was happening.

And also, Dad is going to make me clean up cat poop from now until forever.

Oh well.

CHAPTER 15

The Jewish Tradition

When Friday night Shabbat services are over, we go eat food. This part of Shabbat is called the oneg, and it's my very favorite part. Everyone gathers in a room next to the sanctuary, and the tables are packed with all kinds of delicious desserts.

The moment we get there, I grab a plate and head toward the babka, which is a super-yummy chocolate bread. But Dad taps me on the shoulder. "Rachel, you already had a cookie," he points out.

I guess he's right. I sigh and move away from the table. But I still can't help but look at the babka and imagine what it tastes like. Maya comes over to me. Her plate is full of treats.

"You were so cool!" she tells me in between taking bites of a jelly doughnut.

"Really?"

"Yep!" she says. "Only you would do something like that, Rachel. Plus, your form on the handstand was really good."

I smile. I'm glad someone thought what I did was cool. She even noticed my form! Her nice words almost make the coming cat-poop-palooza worth it.

While Maya talks, someone else comes up to us. I gulp when I see who it is. Rabbi Ellen!

Even though Dad had been talking with one of his grown-up friends, he magically appears next to me the moment Rabbi Ellen arrives. "I am so, so sorry, Rabbi," he says.

He repeats these words three more times. Then Rabbi Ellen interrupts him.

"It's fine. No permanent harm done. But can you do me a favor, Rachel?" Rabbi Ellen asks.

"Yes," I say.

"I'd like for you to not do a handstand in services again. You are an excellent gymnast, but watching you distracts me while I'm leading services, and it distracts other people while they're praying. Do you think you can do that for me?"

I guess she makes sense. I nod at her.

She smiles at me. "Great! And also, I know we all get hungry sometimes. But how about you save the snacks for outside the sanctuary? If you get cookie crumbs all over the sanctuary, the maintenance staff has to clean it up later, and that's not very fair to them."

I hadn't even thought about that, but she's right. I nod again.

"I didn't know there were reasons for all the rules. I'm sorry I distracted everyone and created more work for people."

"Thank you," Rabbi Ellen says. "I appreciate it. By the way, those are most excellent pajamas."

The rabbi likes my pajamas! I'm not surprised. They are extremely cool, after all. Now I remember that the rabbi never did explain why I shouldn't wear them to shul.

Since Rabbi Ellen actually listens to

me, I decide to ask her about it. "I think we should be able to wear pajamas here," I say. "I mean . . . can't we pray in pajamas? Why does it always have to be fancy clothes?"

"Interesting point. I'll think about it. Maybe once in a while, we can do a special wear-your-pajamas-to-shul day. I'd like to wear my pajamas here, too!"

The very thought of the rabbi wearing pajamas makes me giggle. Really, I didn't realize that the rabbi even *has* pajamas! I guess she can't sleep in her regular clothes and yarmulke, though.

"Pajama Day would be soooo awesome," Maya says.

The rabbi grins. "You may have started a real trend, Rachel."

I am a trendsetter! That is so fantabulous.

"You know," Rabbi Ellen adds, "you

could say that questioning rules is part of the Jewish tradition."

"Really?" I ask.

"Absolutely! We have traditions and practices that have been passed down for thousands of years. I guess you could call our traditions rules. But the rules can change over time, and they have. The Talmud is nothing but arguments over rules. We Jews disagree with one another. We look at the Torah, and we make arguments based on the evidence. Maybe we won't ever agree completely with one another, but that's okay. The process of talking it out is very, very Jewish."

I'm practically bouncing up and down. Not only am I a trendsetter, but I am also practicing the Jewish tradition! Now I have even more questions.

"What's the Talmud? I've heard that word before, but I don't know what that is."

The rabbi explains that the Talmud is a book written by rabbis. In the book, they all talk about the Torah. Thousands of rabbis wrote the Talmud over hundreds of years, which is a really, really long time. She says I'll learn more about it in Hebrew school when I'm older. For the first time, I think I might like Hebrew school stuff besides art projects and cooking.

"Rules are important in Judaism, but some rules are more important than others," Rabbi Ellen tells me. "Most grown-ups don't eat on Yom Kippur to observe the holiday. But if someone has a health condition that would make it dangerous for them not to eat all day, they should eat. Protecting and saving a person's life is more important than any other rule, always."

Hmm. That makes sense . . . and it gives me an idea.

"What about cats?" I ask. "Is saving a cat more important than following a rule, too?"

"You could definitely make that argument," Rabbi Ellen says.

I turn toward Dad. He didn't talk much while Rabbi Ellen was explaining things, but I notice him chewing on his lip a whole lot.

"Rachey," he says. "I think we need to talk later. For now, maybe get us both some babka?"

I race off the moment he finishes the question.

CHAPTER 16
The New Rules

The moment we get home, Dad waves me into the living room for an Important Talk. I am really, really not looking forward to it. The last time we had an Important Talk didn't exactly go well. But Cookie is there, and that helps. I find her favorite feather toy and start playing with her while Dad clears his throat.

"I think
I've made a few
mistakes," Dad says.

"Duh!" I say. "You should totally
let me meet Holly Luna."

I mean, this is obvious. But sometimes it takes Dad a while to understand stuff that's obvious. So I just have to be patient with him.

"Yes, well, about that . . ." Dad pauses for a moment. "I was too hard on you, Rachey. Maybe you did break the rules. But you had a reason for it."

"Yes, I did!"

He nods and runs a hand through his hair. "You did. I guess I just got so scared that something bad would happen to you, and I . . . well, I should have been more under-standing of what you did. It's like Rabbi Ellen said. Sometimes there are a whole lot of different rules to think about, and we have to decide which ones are most important. I still do believe in my rule about not crossing the street alone. It's a rule to keep you safe."

I nod.

"But you had a reason for breaking it." He runs a hand through his hair again. "I guess I just want to keep you safe."

"I know," I say, because I do.

"But some rules are more important than others. You were helping Cookie," Dad says.

Wow! Rabbi Ellen must have super-powers. I can't believe she convinced Dad that it's okay to not follow the rules sometimes. I need to give her a big, big thank-you.

"So does this mean I can meet Holly?" I ask. Because that is obviously the most important question.

"Yes," Dad says. "I'll get the tickets tonight."

I jump up from the couch and do a fist pump. "Yay, yay, and yay! Thank you

from the bottom of my heart forever and ever and ever! I guess maybe you're cool after all, Dad."

Dad laughs. Then his face gets all serious again. "I'm glad to hear it. Of course, we still have to discuss today's rule breaking."

Ugh. I knew this was coming, but that doesn't mean I like it.

"Do we have to?" I ask.

"Yes, we do. I understand that you were making a point, but you still disrupted Shabbat services. You know you shouldn't have done that, Rachey."

"Yeah, I know." I make a face. "Does that mean I'm scooping more cat poop?"

"Yep. You're on litter-box duty for the next month."

Ugh. That is a whole lot of cat poop! But it's okay. Because today I learned that you can ask grown-ups about the rules. Sometimes the rules are there for a good reason, and sometimes the rules can change, but no matter what, it's okay to ask questions. And maybe other people will change how they think, too.

So from now on, I will try to follow the rules at shul.

. . . Well, most of the time.

Acknowledgments

Thank you to my editor, Dana Chidiac, for seeing the potential in Rachel's story and working with me to bring it to life. The rest of the team at Macmillan also deserves major kudos. Thank you to Ann Marie Wong, Jean Feiwel, Valery Badio, Alexei Esikoff, Sarah Gompper, Abby Granata, Aurora Parlagreco, Molly Ellis, Mary Van Akin, Mariel Dawson, and Jen Edwards. Every single person who worked on the publicity, school and library marketing,

marketing, and sales teams has my gratitude.

I must also thank my wonderful agent Jennifer Laughran, whose honesty and savvy helped this project from its early stages. Bex Livermore and the rest of the team at Andrea Brown Literary Agency also deserve huge thanks for all the work they do.

An extra-big thank-you to Genevieve Kote, whose vivid illustrations have so perfectly captured the spirit of Rachel and her crew.

Meera Trehan, Adrianna Cuevas, and A. J. Sass all read early versions of this book, providing invaluable feedback and support. Thanks muchly to you, and to the entire community of kidlit authors. Special thanks go to Debbi Michiko Florence and

Meg Eden Kuyatt for your encouragement during the Highlights Foundation chapter book series workshop.

Thanks also to all my friends and family who have supported me through the oftentimes uncertain journey of being a writer. I must give a special shout-out to Jayne Carlin for providing a brilliant suggestion that ended up in the final version.

Many industry professionals, teachers, and librarians have done tireless work so that an unabashedly Jewish chapter book series could be published. Thanks to everyone who has participated in this important and ongoing advocacy.

And finally, thank you to all my readers. I hope you love Rachel as much as I do.